PRAISE FOR *THREE QUARTERS*

Donna Kakonge's new collection of creative non-fiction shows humanity at its best and worst, whether she is depicting malevolent teen boys and girls in the heartless school environs of Cosburn Public School or the quirky loveable family members in St. Vincent. In every story, Donna does not waver from her fearless story telling in which the truth is told at any cost. What results are stories that will make you both laugh and cry. Kakonge's stories never disappoint. – Laura Lush, Governor General's nominee.

Very strong, very vivid writing. I feel as if I am seeing and hearing the events right there in front of my eyes. I like the way Donna captures the language of the child, the young person, then the adult. The stories and writing are unapologetically real. She has a strong, confident style. I just really like her fresh, brave, unvarnished style of writing. – Cynthia Reyes, Author, Communications Expert

From the first chapter, Three Quarters manages to draw you in so that you sympathize with the main character who happens to be the author. She is just ten years old when we first meet her, and both the tone and writing style match her age. The innocent and tender language makes you feel as if this story is crafted by a child. As the young girl ages though, so does the method of expression. Suddenly the writing is too mature to be written by a child. There is a simple description of sitting on a bench at a mall with her siblings and another touching scene describing the day she brought her Dad to class, but then we move closer to current day and a harsher tone as author, Donna Kakonge describes the offensive language she encounters on a bus ride. Stark reality kicks in as she is reminded on that bus ride of a horrible incident from her childhood-Donna's innocence is lost and the writing turns candid. How appropriate that the writing style transitions as the character ages. After all, Three Quarters is about growth and change. It traces the stages of the writer's life, including success and disappointments from childhood to present day. The story is often warm and tender. At other times it is frank. — Teresa Madaleno-Long, Freelance Writer and Media Relations Consultant

THREE QUARTERS

THREE QUARTERS

DONNA KAKONGE

Donna Kay Kakonge, M.A. – Toronto, Ontario, Canada

Three Quarters

First American Edition

Published by Donna Kay Kakonge, MA, ABD, LTD.
Toronto, Canada

Stories Copyright @ 2021 by Donna Kakonge

Amazon Cataloguing

Kakonge, Donna Kay Cindy, author

Three quarters / Donna Kakonge.

ISBN 9798589538656

Editors: Laurie Kallis, John Dunford and Katherine
Kristalovich
Cover Design: Donna Kakonge and Jenny Jamie
Ferenczi

Printed and Bound in the United States

BOOKS AND CDS BY DONNA KAKONGE

How To Write Creative Non-fiction

Totally Unknown Writers Festival Collection 2011

How To Talk To Crazy People: Vignettes of Sixteen Break-down

Young Black Women in Toronto High Schools: Portraits of Family, School and Community Involvement in Developing Goals and Aspirations

For more please visit: http://kakonged.wordpress.com

To my maternal Grandparents:

As a woman who worked as a principal of a school, and a man who was governor of St. Vincent & the Grenadines, as well as worked with the United Nations – You were revolutionaries of your time.

To my paternal Grandparents:

As leaders of your village, and both teachers, you left too soon.

I know you are all some of my foremost angels.

To my Mother for using reverse psychology to get me to write.

To my Father for helping me get my first job at ten years old.

Both of you are the hardest working people I will ever know.

Well, to be perfectly frank with you, I have suffered greatly under racism, but it really hasn't bothered me. Because I feel there are its checks and balances. For every racist, I've found at least ten people who are not racist. And I'm having such a grand time with them that I wasn't worrying with the racists. He's got his problems, he has his high blood pressure, and he has his high cholesterol, he deserves it, let him have it. I was so busy having the friendship, the love and the companion-ship, you saw them here today.

\-   Dr. Carrie Best on her ninety-fourth birthday back in 1994 in Halifax, Nova Scotia, Canada.

This bipolar thing does not seem like such a bad thing.
\-   Sandra Kryzakos, co-host of *Liquid Lunch* on ThatChannel.com in an interview in 2012 with me.

I am nine years old and sitting on a bench at Eglinton Square Mall in East York, Ontario with my brother and sister. My father and mother break up the year before and the three of us kids are living with my mom. We live on Sunrise Avenue, and I have a fifty-dollar bill I find in the hallway to one of the exits of the condo. I marvel at the money, the beautiful crimson red bill. I want to keep it. My mom and dad say to put it in the bank.

My brother, sister and I get tired of waiting in the long line up for the Bank of Nova Scotia, so we are resting on the bench outside the bank in the mall. I have the fifty-dollar bill floating in a plain white plastic bag. The bag with the bill rests to my left, and my brother and sister are on my right.

A middle age white man with balding brown hair sits beside me. I look up at him. I look over at my brother and sister. I feel a tug and with shock, I look back to my left at my hand. The bag is gone, and the man is running into the mall.

The following pages are stories of some of the scams and successful moments, big and small that happen in my life. The big one is an over two hundred thousand dollars loss stemming from a lucky find in the newspaper at the age of thirty-one. These are also stories of how I continue to work my way back financially and continue to fight to keep what I got, and to get more.

ONE

In the early nineteen eighties, I am ten years old and a new vice-principal arrives at my school. At O'Connor Public School in Toronto, Mr. Goldberg sets up a close-circuit television studio. The show us students and Mr. Goldberg produce are called *OCTV News,* short for O'Connor Television News.

In a small room of the school that was a teachers' lounge, an anchor's desk and a camera as big as me replaces coffee makers and plastic cushions. A few grades five students, myself included, rotate through the various production jobs. Sometimes, I am the sound engineer, which means putting the needle on the Beatles song, "Here Comes the Sun," our theme music. Sometimes, I am the announcer, which means telling Angelika to show up to the Peter Pan play rehearsals. She is playing Peter, and I am Wendy.

On International Day we have to bring a dish from our heritage for the other students. Mr. Goldberg forgets it is International Day and didn't write anything into our scripts about it for *OCTV News.* That day I am co-announcing.

"Donna and Eric, just ad-lib about the International Day after the news," Mr. Goldberg says seconds before we go on-air.

Tyrone is the director that day. Standing beside the monstrous camera and facing Eric and I, he holds up his fingers.

"Three, two, one…you're on air," Tyrone says.

Eric and I both investigate the bright red light, trying not to fidget as Mr. Goldberg tells us again and again. Eric and I also try not to keep our heads down as we read from our scripts as Mr. Goldberg also tells us. "Don't rustle the pages," Mr. Goldberg always tells us in our post-show meeting.

The news is first with soccer practice at five o'clock for the girls' and boys' teams. Track and field practice is at five-thirty. Eric announces that the following day on Thursday at lunchtime there will be try-outs for the Easter celebration choir.

After the news Eric asks me what dish I will bring in for International Day on Thursday. I tell him "matoke," a common Ugandan meal made of steamed and mashed green bananas.

"Where is Uganda?" Eric asks.

"In Africa," I say.

"Oh, Africa! I thought they ate people there; I didn't know they ate food!" Eric says.

I almost cry.

"I think there's a lot you don't know about Africa, Eric," I choke out. "My uncles, aunts and cousins who still live there don't eat people."

"Well what is Africa like?" he asks.

I went to Uganda as a baby. I was born and raised in Canada.

My father came to Canada on a Commonwealth scholarship. When he returned to Uganda for a new job with a new wife and baby, that was me, Dictator Idi Amin was in power. We all escaped the country with only our lives.

"Well, Eric…" I pause, feeling the eyes of five hundred other students at O'Connor Public School waiting for me to respond. "My family in Uganda lives in a brick house, not a grass hut. My family in Uganda drives a car, not a camel. My family in Uganda eat matoke, not people."

Silence.

"I didn't know," says Eric.

Eric starts by breaking the silence; however I can hear shouts and screams and cheers from off set in the hallways where TV sets hang high to broadcast the news and I can faintly hear cheering in some of the closer classrooms.

"I want to know more about Uganda," Eric says.

I look up and see Tyrone rolling his hands, giving me the signal that we need to wrap up.

"Tune in for more tomorrow," I say, ad-libbing to the camera. "This is Donna Kakonge and thanks for watching *OCTV News*."

I turn to Eric. "This is Eric Smith and thanks for watching *OCTV News*."

I ask my teacher if my father can come to class and talk about Uganda. Soon afterwards, dad is standing at the front of the class with my globe piggy bank, rattling change as he turns it to point out Uganda.

Later at home, while my father is tucking me into bed he says, "I guess we did feed those kids at O'Connor a lot more than matoke."

THREE

THE COMMERCIAL

My body is exhausted. I work out every day at Trainers Fitness at Bathurst Street and Bloor Street. It is now February and my weight are one hundred and forty-five pounds. That is down from two hundred and eight pounds three months earlier. I am taking my medication every day. I stop smoking. My dad keeps looking at me with a furrow in his eyebrows.

"Are you taking your medication?" my father asks me as I am walking into the door of his house.

"Yes, dad," I answer quickly. "Every day."

"You look like you should see a doctor."

My eyes dart into his dark pupils.

"I do not need to see a doctor. I am fine."

He picks up a brown and red business card sitting on the wood octagon dining room table, with a plastic cloth cover and with small brown and white flowers.

"Here is a card for a doctor that was recommended for you," he says handing me the card. "You should consider seeing him, at least about all of this rapid weight loss."

I look at the card and see the word "psychiatrist." I tear it into jagged pieces and throw it on the dining room table.

"That's it dad!" my back is moving away from him. "I'm going to live with mom."

"You have not been the same since you left Daniel." I hear him say as I pull the door, hard.

I sleep a lot at my mom's, and I miss going to the gym. I am sitting at her kitchen table in Markham, Ontario when she opens the newspaper in front of me.

"Every job I have ever gotten, I got from *Toronto Star*," she says.

I look up at her and then I look at the paper.

There is an ad for a casting company looking for people who have a history of diabetes and Alzheimer's in the family.

"Say if it's a scam, mom?"

She pauses. "Just do not give them any money and I will go with you."

We drive down to Richmond Street and Jarvis Streets in downtown Toronto. Mom is behind the wheel of her burgundy Chevrolet Cavalier because she does not trust me to drive. I left a cigarette hole in the backseat when I was a teenager and she has not let me drive her car since.

"This is the address," she says, parking in the lot. "I will wait outside. If you need me, just run outside. If you take too long, I will go inside."

"Okay, mom."

I kiss her soft brown cheek. The woman is about five feet, seven inches, about three inches shorter than me. Her legs are almost skinny enough to wrap one hand around them. Those coal black eyes can cut anyone like a diamond. I have them too.

Those eyes light up when I am in front of the camera. I am wearing a straight black wig, red lipstick that I buy from Mac and mascara. Since I am not smoking, my teeth look worth all the two thousand dollars my father spent on braces for me when I was a teenager.
The camera goes off, the light and happiness in me goes off.

A tall, dark-haired man, who is lean, tells me that I will be hearing from them in a few days. I pass about seven other women in the waiting area and shrug my shoulders.

My mother is standing outside of the car.

"How did it go?"

"Fine."

"Do you think you got it?"

I step inside the car and put my seatbelt on.
My mom goes to the wheel. "Mom, I don't know. They said they would call in a few days."

She turns the key in the lock of the car. "I will pray, Donna. I will pray for you."

My mom treats me to lunch at Nicey's, a Caribbean restaurant not too far from Markham.

They call. I need to go to Humberview Hospital on the other side of town for the commercial. First, they want to meet with me. I go to Bedford Road, close to OISE/University of Toronto and meet with a tall blonde man who looks like an actor, but he is the one I am signing the contract with. The contract is confusing, however according to the contract I am going to receive about two hundred and six thousand dollars in residuals. I sign.

My dad is so happy that he drives me to the commercial. He needs to work on his houses, so he tells me I need to take the bus back.

I look the same as I did for the audition. The nice make up lady does not even touch me. Since I am wearing a wig, the hairstylist need not touch me either. I just wait in a room that looks as though it is a locker room for nurses until the director calls me in and I chat with the hairstylist.
They give me an orange sweater to wear with a V-neck. They hand me a script and I can't even read it. I find the language awkward to say. The director hands the script back to the writer and in moments, a clean and simple script is done in about five minutes that is easy to say. It takes three takes. I am done. *My fifteen minutes of fame over*, I think.
By noon, I am heading out of Humberview Hospital and try to catch a bus home. Once I reach my mom's, a kind woman named Karen who works with the casting company tells me the director and casting company are so pleased with me they also want me to do a photo shoot that will be spread throughout the TTC. That half day shoot that happens about a week later is two hundred and fifty dollars in pay.

My friend Cyril wants to congratulate me. It is a mild early March evening and Cyril does a lot of acting. The commercial is on the air, all the time, but I am not being paid yet.

Now, just like when I was in high school, I live part-time at my mom's and part-time at my dad's so I can exercise at Trainer's Fitness again.

"Donna," Cyril says. "You should join ACTRA." ACTRA is the Association of Canadian Television and Radio Artists.

"Why?"

"You would make more money."

He sits beside me at a rooftop bar in Yorkville sipping his beer slowly.

"More?"

"Yes."

The next day, my mom lets me borrow her car to drive down to the ACTRA office. I join ACTRA. Cyril is wrong. I end up getting three thousand dollars for the half day I spent on camera with the commercial as an apprentice member. Doing the math…that is less than two hundred and six thousand dollars!

LESSONS

My mom's place is too far, so I move in with my dad full-time again. I'm back at Trainer's Fitness full-time too.

I am not feeling very well. I start getting strange thoughts that people are stalking me and people want to steal the little money I have. More stable work is harder to come by. I get the freelance gigs here and there; however, I am still waiting to be paid by ACTRA and my dad thinks I am crazy for joining ACTRA and breaking a great contract. I do bit parts for the W Network and the Food Network.

I go to see the doctor that is torn in pieces on my dad's dining room table.

He puts me on two mood stabilizers at once. I flip into mania. I end up at Toronto General Hospital.

DECIDING TO STOP

I start by opening a glass of red Woodbridge wine. Three pink pills rest to my right on my African unity table with its glass top in front of me. First, I pour the wine, slowly, into a Dollarstore clear wine glass. My black Panasonic cordless phone blares as the tip of the glass touches my lips.

Glass in hand, I pick up the phone.

"Donna!" I recognize Diane's voice. "Let's go out drinking tonight!"

"I have already started," I laugh as I reply. "Where do you want to go?"

"Let's go to Gem's," Diane says. "I'll come pick you up in ten minutes."

Diane lives in Wychwood, a neighborhood north of mine in Toronto.

I am wearing a plain black tank top and dark blue Gap jeans. This is what I plan to wear to bed as well. When I had my sixteenth nervous breakdown and with God's prayers my last, I had just left the Toronto General Hospital. After, I lived in a shelter for two weeks before I moved to a West Lodge apartment in Parkdale for fourteen months.

Before I put the Woodbridge back in the fridge, I hear Diane's horn of her red and rusty Mazda just outside my ground floor basement apartment. I grab my house keys; I grab my pills and dry swallow them before I exit the door. Diane and I go to Gem's.

That night, I drink so much at Gem's; vodka and cranberry juice, vodka and orange juice, Heineken, I try Jamaican rum for the first time, and I take my first shots of tequila. The drinks are cheap.

I heave yellow liquid all over Gem's floor. Diane drives me back home. At night, I dream I am having another breakdown.

On the next weekly Thursday appointment with my psychiatrist, I speak to her about what happened and about my dream.

"You know," she starts. "The medication works better when you don't drink."

Since that day in early 2004, I do not drink alcohol, not even cough syrup.

PHONE SEX

I move from my addiction to alcohol to a brief addiction to phone sex. Diane introduces me to chat lines.

"You can meet really great guys on the phone," Diane says as she hands me *Now Magazine*. "You don't have to do anything with them if you don't want. Just chat with them. You don't even have to talk about sex. These are just lonely guys looking for hot chicks to talk to."

Diane and I are sitting in her car in the Faema Café parking lot close to Christie Street and Dupont Avenue in Toronto. Diane works at The Beer Store and constantly complains to me about her job. She is forty years old and I am thirty two. I do freelance radio for the Canadian Broadcasting Corporation and can barely pay my bills. Diane can relate to that.

Diane just moved to Toronto from Vancouver. She left an abusive relationship with the man she went out there with five years ago. She now goes out on dates every night and says it is because of this chat line.

My last relationship with Daniel was supposed to end up in marriage. I have been single for almost a year now.

"Diane," I say. "I cannot do this alone. Can you be at my place when I make the first call?"

Diane always sounds drunk. I think it is probably from the second-hand alcohol fumes at The Beer Store.

"You don't need me to be at your house, Donna."

"Why not? I am a little scared."

Diane reaches for a thermos between her legs at the driver's seat and takes a sip. "There is nothing to be scared of."

I shrug, I look at my watch. It is seven-thirty and I am thinking if I am going to do this, I do not want it to be too late. My psychiatrist encouraged me to go to bed early.

"Okay, Diane," I put the seatbelt buckle back on. "I want to go home."

"Are you going to call?"

"Yeah," I say quietly.

Diane takes another swig of her thermos.

"What is that any way?" I ask Diane pointing to the thermos.

"It's just coffee."

Diane puts on her seatbelt and turns her key fast in the ignition. The Mazda is standard, and I know how to drive a standard car, but Diane would not ever allow me to drive the Mazda. I could see her gearing into reverse and then she slams her foot on the accelerator.

Metal crashes.

Silence.

"Oh my God," I say breaking the seconds of still air. "Diane, you hit a car!"

Without saying anything, Diane gears into drive with almost the full speed of the car and races out of the parking lot.

"Diane, my God," I say as she is driving me home. "You should have at least left a note."

"What for?" She says angrily. "That wasn't my fault."

"The car was parked!" I say.

Diane says nothing until she drops me home.

"Just make sure you call, Donna. You're love life is dry." Diane chuckles in her throaty ex-smoker laugh out the rolled down window as she drives away.

I stand outside my door before entering. I look at the snow on the ground. *Diane is a very bad and crazy person;* I think to myself – *Why am I the one seeing a psychiatrist every week?*

FIRST TIME LUCKY

I open *Now Magazine* before I go to bed and find an ad for a chat line that has a green and purple logo. Not knowing what I am in for, I dial.

A crazy female voice comes on and asks me to choose if I am a man or a woman. I press woman. Then, it asks whether I want a fling, a date, a causal relationship, or a long-term relationship. I press long-term relationship. Diane's life is too crazy for me. I do not need to go to the nut bin again for anyone or anything. My mama tells me so.

"See who is on chat now!" The voice says. "You can choose who you want to talk to and have an intimate, one-on-one conversation."

I listen to the male voices. It is only near the end when I hear this deep, rich, beautiful voice that sounds as though he is a radio announcer. I press that one.

"Hello?" He says quickly before I even have a chance to reenergize my courage. "Hello?"

"Yes," I say.

"What is your name?" He asks.

"Donna."

"I'm Sean."

Hmm, I think, *that is a nice name.*

"When is your birthday?" He asks.

"August twelfth, 1972," I reply. *This guy sounds like fun,* I think. "When is your birthday?"

"July twenty seventh, 1956," he says quickly. "Do you work?"

"I do freelance radio," I say.

"You have a beautiful voice," he says.

"So do you," I answer. "That's why I chose you," I venture.

"I'm glad you did," he says. "What do you look like?"

I hesitate. I look myself up and down.

"I'm tall, thin…I'm black," I'm worried he won't want to talk to me anymore. "You don't sound black."

"No, I'm not," he says, and I can hear the smile in his voice. "I love black women and I am Irish. My eyes are blue. My hair is blonde."

I shift on my patterned green sofa. *Well, what's next?*

"Where do you live?" He asks without a break in the conversation.

"I live downtown."

"So do I," he says. "Can I come over to your place?"

I think of my dad next door. *What would he think?* I would not want him thinking I am anything like Diane.

"Well," I start. "We can't have sex. I am on my period." *Which is true.*

"That's fine," he says deeply. "I just want to see you. I just want to talk to you."

The feeling of being overwhelmed leaves me a little.

"Where do you work?" I ask him.

"Donna, I work for the government." He says.

Well, CBC is a crown corporation. "I guess I do too." I say.

He laughs. "Do you work for the CBC?"

"Yes," I reply.

"I listen to CBC Radio a lot."

I nod my head and fall silent.

When he asks me for my address, I give it to him. He arrives at my door in literally ten minutes.

We are the same height. He is wearing light blue jeans and a vertically striped dress shirt. He tells me I am beautiful. He is older, but in good shape and I tell him I like his eyes. I show him around my apartment. He says it is nice. While he is in the washroom, I step outside for a cigarette and see his cute cherry red Toyota parked in my car port. I enter smelling like smoke.

"I didn't know you smoke," he says. "You shouldn't."

"I know," I say, putting the Gauloises yellow pack on the Salvation Army wooden table beside my door I got for five dollars back in Montréal. "I'm trying to stop."

"I can help you," he says. "My dad died of cancer."

"I'm sorry to hear that," I say sincerely.

"He was a big smoker," he says looking at the pack of cigarettes.

I look at the clock above my sofa. It is almost ten and I have not taken my medication.

"I should be going to bed now."

"Do you have bipolar disorder?" he asks.

I am shocked to stillness. *How did he know? No one had ever asked me that. They only know when I tell them.*

I nod my head. "I guess you want to leave." I say.

"No, no," he says. He sits down. "I work for the Ministry of Community and Social Services. I administer ODSP to people."

"What's ODSP?" I ask.

"It's the Ontario Disability Support Program," he says. "We give money to people who have disabilities if they cannot work. You are lucky you are working. When is the last time you were in the hospital?"

"Last year," I say grimly. "It will be my last time."

He nods his head.

"How did you know? Do I seem crazy?" I ask. "Maybe it was crazy for me to let you come here."

"No, no," he starts, and I am taking in every one of his words. "I saw your medication in the bathroom, and I know many psychiatrists usually prescribe that for bipolar disorder."

I nod my head.

"I would not have known," he says. "You seem lucid."

"Well," I say heading to the bathroom to get my medication. "I am when I take my meds."

Sean sits silently on my couch while I am in the bathroom swallowing my pills with bathroom water. *I forgot to hide these pills before he came. He came over so bloody fast. Now he is going to think I am some crazy he needs to take care of. I don't need to be taken care of.*

"Are you done?" he asks as I reenter the living room.

"Yes," I reply.

"Do you take vitamins too?"

"No," I say. "I used to a long time ago, but they're expensive. I don't make enough money for that."

"Cut out smoking and you could afford to do that," Sean says.

We talk, or argue, all night long. *I really like him.* Before he leaves, he asks me to marry him. He lives just up the street.

SEAN

I decide not to marry Sean when Diane says he is too old for me.

"He'll die before you for sure," she says.

When I tell Sean my decision, he is okay with it.

It is winter and Sean takes me to repertory movie theatres throughout Toronto. We see a movie every week. He takes me walking through High Park in the snow and introduces me to his sister and her family who live close by. Later, Sean introduces me to his mother, the woman I have heard so much about. She is dressed in an immaculate yellow suit and looks like a skinnier version of the Queen of England. She lives in uptown Toronto and we drive over to the west end, which Sean prefers and eat hamburgers with fries at a Fire Pit close to Kipling subway station. Sean drives me through the Bridle Path, one of the wealthiest neighborhoods in Toronto and shows me his old house. His old house, which is a good size house, is dwarfed by the multi-room mansions close by and with king-size swimming pools in the backyards.

I am not alone ever, any night of the week. On the weekends, Sean heads up north to a spiritual group he is involved with that believe in Buddhism. Sean is a Buddhist. He also believes that when a man has an ejaculation during sex, he loses his strength and sex should only be for procreation. In all the two years that I know Sean, we have sex once. It is the first time I have an orgasm from the inside of my vagina without stimulating myself.

Sean and I spend a wonderful two years together. By this time, I am no longer with the CBC. I am laid off by the summer of 2004 and I start doing freelancing for Media Research Institute as a car journalist. At the same time, I take a bilingual receptionist job with the Ontario Women's Directorate in the fall of 2004 to make extra money. Sean constantly complains about Toronto and about how loud and crowded it is. He is applying to jobs just outside of Toronto.

"I want to live in Whitby," he tells me. "We can live together. Houses are cheaper out there."

"I don't want to live in Whitby," I say. "I like Toronto. I like living downtown. Say if I couldn't get a job in Whitby?"

"I'll take care of you," he says.

This is what I feared all along.

So, we do not end up in an argument, I say nothing. By the end of the year, Sean finds a job with the same government department in Whitby. He moves there and we try to have a long-distance relationship. He is living in the basement of a female friend's house and complains that it is infested with rats. By time my bilingual receptionist job turns into a bilingual grants' consultant job with the Ontario Women's Directorate, Sean starts calling about once a month and then once every two months. When I try to reach him on the weekends, he is always heading up north.

There is a French language test I need to receive a superior competency level with so I can get my job with the government to be permanent. At that time, the government does not deem my French superior. I leave the directorate saying a tearful goodbye to the friendly and close group of twenty-nine others who still have their job in the office. At least I did not lose my work with the Media Research Institute.

When I tell Sean, he begs me to move to Whitby. By this time, Diane moves in with her mother after she is fired from The Beer Store and she is no longer a distraction. I consider it, but I have always been a downtown girl. Plus, when it comes to begging, I am the one who needs to beg Sean to have sex with me and he stands firm to his Buddhist philosophies.

Just as I am about to give in because I am so lonely and broke, I receive an email from my long-time friend Darcy from the CBC that changes my life. To this day, I cannot fathom why she sent that God saving email?

THE COACH

Hi Donna,

I hope everything is great in your world. I heard you were no longer working for the CBC and I left there too. I started seeing a career coach named John Hurt and he was helpful to get me into other journalism work. He has more than forty years of experience in journalism and I thought I would send this to you in case it may help you. He does charge, he would see you about once a week, but it is not much money. I recommend him because he changed my life. Here is his email:

thecoach@gmail.com.

Good luck!

Darcy

P.S. Please do let me know how it goes if you decide to work with him.

Minutes after I receive the email, I email John Hurt. I heard of him.

Dear Mr. Hurt:

I received your email from Darcy Kaso about your career coaching services. I would be interested in starting this with you as soon as possible. Perhaps we can better discuss where I am in my career when we meet. Where and when would be the best place and time to meet?

Sincerely,

Donna Kakonge

www.donnakakonge.com

An hour later, John Hurt emails:

John comes over to my place later that week. I find out that he is working freelance as a radio writer with the CBC, as well as teaching journalism at Centennial College. I tell him I want to write again. I got a short story published in *Headlight Anthology* with Concordia University. This is my true passion. I also tell him I want to teach again. I taught at Carleton in Ottawa as a teaching assistant for two years, as well as taught at Makerere University in Kampala, Uganda and at Concordia University in Montréal. This is also my true passion.

He gives me advice that I should check out all the magazines and newspapers that I want to write for and approach them with story ideas. He gives me some tips on how to do it, or rather reminds me of things I learned in journalism school at Carleton. He also recommends that I start approaching some of the schools and colleges in town to teach.

"Since you have your master's degree in media studies," he says, "It should be easy for you to find teaching work. A lot of colleges and universities are asking for master's degrees, especially the colleges. A lot of the universities you do need a PhD."

"I have thought of doing my PhD too," I say. "Actually, my dad has one in biology from the University of Waterloo and I have wanted to do one since I was in high school."

I used to have *Dr. Donna Kay Cindy Kakonge* flashing across my IBM desktop computer when I was a teen.

"What would you want to do your PhD in?" John asks. "They can be costly and there are a lot of out of work PhDs."

"Well, maybe communication studies, but I don't particularly enjoy the theory," I say. "I used to have to read Heidegger four times translated from the German to English to understand that guy. He would write sentences often four lines long or even longer."

"Well, just see how it goes," John says. He looks at his watch. "Time's up. Did you like our first coaching session?"

"I loved it!" I tell him.

"I told you that you would love me," he says with a grin.

"Well, how much would I have to pay you from now on?"

"You told me how much you make," John says. "Would thirty dollars an hour once a week fit into your budget? I don't want to break your bank."

"That should be fine," I say. *Actually, he is very reasonable.*

"Great!" He says standing up and heading to the door. "I have a hockey game to go to."

"You watch hockey?" I ask. "I used to watch hockey with my boyfriend Sean every Friday night."

"I play hockey."

I look at him. The man is at least sixty years old.

"Yes," he says still grinning. "An old dog can have new tricks. Plus, I have played hockey my whole life. I was part of one of the first Negro hockey leagues in Montréal where I was born."

"Cool," I say.

John Hurt is cool and reasonable.

TEACHING/WRITING

Thanks to John encouraging me to check out magazines I want to write for, I start writing with *New Dreamhomes and Condominiums Magazine*. I was at the bus stop at Spadina Avenue and Dupont Street heading west to go home when I check out the magazines in this light blue box. I pick up *New Dreamhomes* and read it from cover-to-cover as soon as I get home. The email for the editor is on the masthead, so just as John advised, I send her a pitch about doing a rags-to-riches story about people who make a fortune with real estate and attach my resume.

She emails me back saying she likes the idea but will pass on it. She ends with letting me know there is a project called Options for Homes that allows people who can only afford a small down payment on a home to own one. She just got the press release when my email came in and she would like to know if I want to do the story.

I jump at it. I take two buses plus the subway to get out to the downtown east end where Options for Homes is headquartered. I use a digital camera I buy at a pawn shop that John suggests I go to in order to get "my gear" as he says. *Dreamhomes* uses my story and one of my pictures. It is a front-page story the following week. They pay me two hundred dollars promptly two weeks later.

Sean is excited for me. He even shows the article to his mom and his sister. We still speak about once a month, sometimes six weeks, sometimes eight weeks. He told me long ago I could date other people, but I have not done that. He says he is not dating anyone else either.

I keep writing for *Dreamhomes*, then *Pride Newsmagazine* that focuses on the African Canadian community, then *Canadian Newcomer*. All this time, I am also still working as a car journalist with the Media Research Institute. Despite the money coming in, I am still having a problem paying my bills.

My friend Mark suggests since I used to model, now that I am older, I should get into art modeling. I go online and find a list of all of the art schools in Toronto. I email every single one. By the following week, I am modeling for Max the Mutt Animation school, The Toronto School of Art, Durham College and borrow my dad's car to get out there, The Arts & Letters Club, The Forest Hill Community Centre and even land a modeling gig at a small Korean community center in Toronto. I ask for the nude sketch of myself from the artist whose work I like the best at the Korean community center and purchase a silver-colored frame for it at Sears inside the Eaton Centre.

By the summer of 2005, John comes to our session with the *Toronto Star* in his hand. He is holding the careers section.

"Centennial College where I still teach is hiring a full-time professor," he tells me. "You should apply."

I am excited. I read the job advertisement carefully. John reads it for me again out loud.

"The deadline is coming up soon," he says. "I don't know if that means they have someone in mind or not. I may be on the hiring committee."

I almost pee in my pants. "Does that mean I have the job?"

"No, it really doesn't," he says. My face falls. "There is a lot of competition for these jobs. They pay well. If you know what you are doing, it is relatively easy work. It just means that at least they will know who you are and who knows what can come out of it."

I apply.

I wait.

I wait a long time.

In the meantime, I respond to an advertisement on Craigslist for a job to write curriculum for an online course. I meet a beautiful, young, blond man who is running an online school. He wants to have a writing course as part of the courses offered and hires me to write the curriculum. He wants the entire curriculum to be something his students can read online and do their homework online as well. This is how I come to write *How to Write Creative Non-fiction*. When the curriculum is done, the young man disappears and does not ever pay me. I am surfing the Internet and find a site called Lulu.com where you can self-publish a book for free and have an online store. I wait on this too until the following year.

I do not get the job, but when the dean of the School of Communication, Media and Design at Centennial College calls to let me know, he tells me they would be interested in hiring me part-time. I just need to contact the coordinator of the journalism program.

The coordinator is a wonderful person. He has experience with American television, having worked for NBC, the National Broadcasting Corporation in the United States. His name is Sean too, but married. He tells me there is a new program between Centennial College and the University of Toronto Scarborough (UTSC) campus offering a diploma in journalism coupled with a bachelor's degree from UTSC where the student chooses to specialize in a particular area. I would be paid by Centennial College, however also working with university undergraduate students. He would like for me to start teaching magazine journalism for the winter semester of 2006.

Finally! After five years of trying to get work in teaching since I left teaching English as a Second Language in Montréal in 2001, I am teaching again. I did have a job with Young People's Press back in 2002 where I was working with high school students, but my forced vacation by my former fiancé to South Africa put a stop to that job. I was finally going to be in my element again.

Sean at Centennial College let me know about the job in September of 2005. In October, November and December, I work and hang out with Julie, my Malaysian friend who writes for the CBC Online. We go for coffee and walks in our neighborhood. She lives in the Annex close to where I live. I also continue to see John Hurt every week since I am still planning to make more money than what I am seeing come in. My psychiatrist appointments move from once a week to once every two weeks. I continue to stop drinking and the last drink I had was that night at Gem's in 2004 with Diane. I do not ever hear from Diane with her final words to me being: "I don't think you can help me." Julie is a far more motivated and pleasant friend. Once a month, I talk to Sean who lives in Whitby and wonder if I should marry him.

SELF-PUBLISHING/TEACHING

I have thirty students in my class. The first class goes well and Sean, the coordinator at Centennial asks me to return in the fall to teach beat reporting and note-taking and composing for journalists.

By the summer of 2006, I contact the coordinator of Seneca College and they hire me for the fall of 2006 to teach media writing. That summer, I finally publish *How To Write Creative Non-fiction*, and about three weeks later I publish my master's thesis originally called *Afro Forever*, but I decide I prefer the title *What Happened to the Afro?* after doing a story about hair weaves for *Pride Newsmagazine*.

In December of 2006, I have an interview at Humber College. The coordinator, Dan, remembers me from the CBC. We used to work together. I was an editorial assistant at the time, and he was a producer. His co-worker, Ann, teaches at Humber and is doing her PhD at Charles Sturt University in Australia online. They both hire me to teach radio broadcasting starting January 2007. That year, I return to the CBC to do a story for Radio Canada International based in Toronto.

I stay at Centennial for six years, Seneca for four years, Humber and the University of Guelph-Humber for two years, Trebas Institute for two years, George Brown College and Ryerson University for a semester. In 2009, I return to the CBC Radio to the CBC on a volunteer basis as part of a Seneca College committee to find out how Seneca can work with the CBC. In May of 2010, I start my doctorate degree at OISE/University of Toronto where I work as an Academic Advisor. I also work for Yorkville University and Florida

University of Health and Sciences doing online teaching. In September of 2012, I started an online law degree with the University of London International Programmes. In May of 2013, I officially start teaching Self-Publishing Around the World with the University of Toronto (U of T) School of Continuing Studies. For January of 2014, I start teaching Broadcast Writing with U of T's School of Continuing Studies.

TV PARTIES

Beep! I glance over the lower right-hand corner of my laptop to see the email that comes in January of 2011. It is my sister Karen:

Hey Donna,

I just remembered that Aunt Lillie, Jackie and her boyfriend are supposed to come by and visit this afternoon, around one thirty. I guess dad wanted to host them here because it's cleaner. You are welcome to come by and visit too. It would be nice to see them again and to meet Jackie's boyfriend!

Karen

"Really great people make you feel that you, too, can become great."

— Mark Twain

I live next door to my dad in a laneway in Toronto. My sister is pregnant for the second time, her husband and my niece, live on the next avenue. It is not far to get over to my sister's house, but the January weather in Toronto is brutal this year.

Last year, 2010, had been a mild winter. This year, 2011, had "bursts of arctic air" as Chris Potter always says on CP24 and many long and snowy days. The laneway rarely gets shoveled, except for my dad and a few other diligent neighbors. I have not yet decided if I will go over to my sister's place. Sunday afternoon comes and my dad calls me while I am in the office of my ground floor basement apartment to tell me his sister arrived.

I am in the middle of working on a project for school so I listen to the message he leaves.

"I hope you can come," he says on my internal Bell machine.

I quickly finish with my assignment for school and decide to go. I put on my grey coat with a hole in the right shoulder and with a sparkly purple broach I received from my former professor from Carleton University Mr. Frajkor for Christmas 2010. I have not showered yet for the day and it is past three in the afternoon. I slide on my outdoor shoes for my carport and trudge through the snow, down the slushy laneway, up the driveway slope and around the bend to reach the sidewalk leading to my sister's house.

After I ring the bell, I can hear the familiar running of my niece Oshun to the door. She will be four in March and the minute I receive her smiles and hugs I am glad I have come.

The KFC that is cold and the cans of Five Alive and Coca-Cola are spread out for self-serve in the kitchen. Later, once collected by my aunt, cousin, her boyfriend and me, the food is spread out on my sister's dining room table.

Football is on TV and my dad sits slouched on my sister's cream leather sectional with his beer belly protruding and watching the game. Once my Aunt Lillie is done her meal, she goes to sit close to my dad and watches football.

"You like the game?" my sister asks our Aunt Lillie.

"Oh yes," she says. "I don't miss a game."

Oshun sits beside her mother who is in her rocking chair and casts her eyes down.

Felix, Jackie's new boyfriend, stays seated at the dining room table across from me. I come to find out that he works for the TTC, Toronto Transit Commission and met my cousin Jackie at Ryerson while studying business and Jackie is still in nursing school.

"Wanna come see my room, Auntie Donna?" asks Oshun tugging at my sweater.

"Sure," I say.

We climb the stairs to her room which is the closest one to the top floor. I look around and notice the added crib.

"Who keeps this room so clean?" I ask.

"I do!" Oshun says. She leans into whisper to me. "Mommy and Daddy help of course."

She points to the crib.

"And this is where the baby is going to sleep."

"Oh, that's good. It will be good for you to have someone to play with."

"Yeah," she says smiling.

My sister Karen calls up from downstairs.

"Oshie, how about you have something to eat?"

Oshun and I descend the carpeted stairs slowly, with me keeping an eye on her from behind while she takes them step by step on her bum.

"But I'm not hungry," she gets to the bottom and looks at the TV. "I want to watch my shows."

"You can watch them after everyone leaves," my sister says.

I say my goodbyes to everyone, excusing myself for having a lot of work to do and stand by the entrance putting on my coat while Oshun sits at her child's table in the kitchen nook.

"Auntie Donna, I want to watch my shows."

I slip on my shoes and call out to my sister.

"Karen, can't Oshun watch her shows?"

"She can watch them after everyone leaves. Don't get caught up in her drama. She is very good at advocating for herself."

I can hear the laughter from the other family members inside. I look at Oshun who has her head in her hands and her elbows rest on the white table.

"I'm sorry, Oshie. I tried. I'll try harder next time."

"Thank you, Auntie Donna."

I leave the house with my eyes tearing.

THE PARTY

Susan Miller's Astrologyzone.com is calling for Friday the thirteenth of 2012 to be a good date night for Leos. I think about this all day as I also enjoy my day off work.

I have two failed attempts at setting up dates. After that, I call my friend Tiffany who lives down the street.

"Hi, Donna," she says with her usual gleeful voice competing with Virgin Radio on my stereo, with a record player and two cassette decks. Her sound tinged with a British accent and I know the voice since I was at Carleton University doing my journalism degree. "How are you?"

"This week has been busy," I start. "My TA work is more hours than I had thought, however I did have an inkling of that before I started. I guess it is true that 'idle hands make devil's work.'" I smile into the phone. "I have been able to keep out of trouble and have fun at the same time."

"Marvelous!" Tiffany says. "How are things going with school?"

"Good. I still need to work on my thesis proposal. One of my committee members really helped me to focus on my research questions and she thinks if I get my proposal in by the end of this month, I can start my research in April."

"That is great," Tiffany says. I can hear her TV in the background.

"Tif, how are things going with you?"

"Things are really good," she says. "I'm going to an office party tonight on Elm Street...some place called Oro I think," she laughs. "We can eat and drink all we want."

"Oh, you have plans."

"No...what is it?"

"I wanted to go out dancing."

"You!" Tiffany raises her voice. "I'm surprised. Don't you usually go to bed early?"

"I can stay up," I say seriously. "I really want to go out dancing."

There is a pause while I figure Tif is thinking.

"Well, I will already be downtown," she says. "I can call you at ten and if that is not too late, we can go out after that."

"Perfect!" I say. "Tif, thanks so much. You are the perfect person to go out dancing with. It has been a long time since I have been out dancing."

"Good. It'll be fun. I will call you at ten. I better go. I am already late for the office party."

"Okay, Tif. Thanks so much. I will see you at ten."

She hangs up. I look at the clock. It is about seven-fifteen.

I look down at my clothes. I have black Adidas leggings on and my feet, yellow crocs, Calvin Klein black socks, a Roots sweatshirt in grey with the words "Roots" in red and white and my hair has not been combed in about a day.

I go to my treadmill and lift off the ten-pound kettle weights in grey, yellow and white and place them on my café table in my kitchen. My pink and white sneakers I get from my sister are sitting on top of the treadmill belt and I pick them up, kick off my crocs and put them on. I turn up the volume to Virgin and get the safety key from a drawer for the treadmill. I rev up to two point one and walk for twenty minutes. After, I take off all my clothes, turn the taps to a warm shower and step inside my bathtub to shower.

I use my power toothbrush, floss and use my plastic toothpicks for my gums. I use Exact baby's cream for my skin and face and Burt's Bees for my lips. I stand just outside of the bathroom, blankly looking to my left, thinking of what is in that closet there, then looking to my right, thinking of what the closet is there.

I turn left first. I pull out my red Kaliyana shirt and pull it over my head. I walk in the south direction of my apartment, where if you are outside you can see the CN Tower not that far away and grab my Ricki's black slacks with the white pinstripes. I pull on my dark brown Keen boots, drape a purple scarf around my neck and put my yellow prescription eyeglasses on. I look at myself in the mirror.

I look at the time. It is eight o'clock. I have time. I put on my coat and go outside, pulling the door in and sitting down on the white chair outside with a black astray behind my right shoulder. I pull my Gauloises out of my pocket and light it with a red lighter, the only one I have working.

The streetlamp in the laneway flickers like a candle in the wind. My neighbour June has her festive lights on and I stare at the pretty colors, thankful they are helping me to think.

After two cigarettes, I go back inside. I check my email. I look in the mirror again. My hair…I go to my southeast closet and pull out my afro puff. I go into the bathroom and slick my hair back with aloe vera gel and then attach the afro puff with a pull string. I hide the string in my hair and look at myself in the mirror again.

I go out for another smoke. I come back to the mirror. One of my favourite songs by Usher is playing, *Without You.*

I go back to the bathroom and look under the sink. I find my makeup bag. The black bag looks grey from the dust.

I pull out my Mac lipstick and mirror that were a gift from Sean six years ago.

Ignoring professional makeup artist's advice that you should not wear makeup longer than two years old; I use the brush to paint the cranberry color to my lips. I smooth my eyebrows down with some sweat on my fingertips.

The lipstick is on my lips for so long, when I add the shimmery silver other half of the Mac tube, the cranberry paint has dried to my lips, the canvas. I smoke another cigarette and add more cranberry and silver on.

I go into the living room and look at the clock above my red leather sofa. It is now ten o'clock. I look at the phone. I go outside. Tif is probably a little late. Ten minutes later, she calls.

"Tif!"

"Donna," she says, sounding drunk. "Sorry I'm a little late. I got into a conversation with someone from work and…"

"Do not worry about it," I say. "I figured as much. Do you still want to go? I am ready. I have my coat on and everything."

"Yes, I still want to go," she says. "I'm on Elm Street. It's close to Bay."

"Do not worry," I say. "I know where it is. I'll be there by about ten forty-five. I will call you on your cell when I am outside the restaurant. Oro, right?"

"Yes, that's it."

"See ya."

I hang up the phone.

I jump into my silver 2011 Volkswagen Golf on lease from Don Valley Volkswagen and get to Christie and follow the fastest route I know down to Elm Street. I get there at about 10:35 p.m.

I call Tif on my cell and she asks me to wait while she is inside the restaurant.

"Okay, Tif. I will be smoking outside."

We decide to go to the entertainment district. I find an affordable place to park and Tif and I split the cost of parking. The parking attendant looks familiar.

PARKING LOT

The parking attendant looks familiar. It is not just because I saw him a year ago when I parked at the same lot. Then, I was going to The Totally Unknown Writers Festival at the Rivoli on Queen Street West in Toronto. I read my story "Lizard in the Yard" early enough in the show while most people were sober. Tonight, I was out to party!

"Eh, I remember you," the parking attendant says. "Where did you disappear to?"

"I'm out partying tonight with my friend," I say. "I have not been out dancing in about eight years!"

"Wow," he says. Tif murmurs too. "That is a long time."

"Where are you from?" Tif asks. "Are you from Ghana?"

The parking attendant rubs his chin with his left hand. "Around those parts..."

Tif leans over me from the passenger seat and takes a better look at him in the booth.

"Ethiopia? Eritrea?" She continues.

"Around those parts," he repeats.

"Where are the good places to go around here?" I ask him. "I was going to take my friend to Cake, but it is a far walk in this cold. Is there anywhere that is good that is closer?"

"Go to City," he says. "Go to City. They play dance music there."

"Good music?" I ask.

"Depends on what you want," he starts. "Do you want a mixed crowd? Go to City. If you go on Richmond Street, it is seventy-five percent black."

"A mixed crowd sounds nice," I say and Tif nods her head.

"How much is parking?" Tif asks. "I've got this, Donna," she whispers to me.

I look down at the yellow and red price list board and see twenty dollars.

"It's twenty dollars," he says.

I look up at him. "How long have you been working here?" I ask.

He looks at me with a smile. "A long, long time."

He sighs.

"I think I know you from way back," I say. "I used to park here when I worked at the CBC down the street."

He stares.

"I remember you," he says. "We get a lot of celebrities around here. I've met Denzel Washington and Dwayne somebody is my friend. George Stro...stro..."

"Stroumboulopoulos," I say.

"Yes," he says. "He is my friend too."

"Do you mean Dwight Drummond?" I ask.

"Yes," he says. "Dwight Drummond is a long-time friend of mine since he was working at CITY."

"What did you do at the CBC?" he asks.

"Lots of things," I say. I point to Tif. "Tiffany worked there too. We used to work together at Radio Canada International in Montréal."

"This is it," he says. "Where did you go? How long were you in Montréal?"

"Almost five years."

"Let's pay the man," says Tif with a smile.

Tif hands me a twenty-dollar bill and I give her back a ten-dollar bill.

"We'll split the parking," I say.

"I want to treat you tonight Donna," Tif says. "I just got paid."

I shake my head. "We'll see about that."

"So, your name is Donna?" the parking attendant asks.

"Yes," I say. "What is yours?"

"My name is Dima," I hear.

"Dima?"

"No, Gima," he says.

"Gima," I pause. "That's a nice name."

I hand over the money.

"When did you start working here?" I ask. "I mean what year?"

"Oh," he pauses. "I guess about 1995 or so. I was in Germany before that."

"I've been there," I say. "I have probably known you all that time. I would park at this lot for my night shifts at the Corp. because it was cheaper than any other lot in the area."

He smiles at me. "I should have got your number then."

"Are you married?" I ask hopefully.

He nods his head.

"Yes," I say. "You should have got my number then."

"Let's go," says Tif. "I need to use the washroom. The alcohol I drank at the office party is going through me."

"Bye, Gima."

"Bye, Donna."

PHYSICAL SURPRISES

The appointment to have my physical with Toronto Western Hospital's Family Health team is in August of 2012. A day before, I complain to them the doctor is male and I do not want to go.

"Dr. Toussaint is a woman," the female receptionist says to me over the phone.

I feel anger. "Well, I did not know that," I say. "No one there even told me if my doctor was male or female. My first appointment was with a man and I just thought it was with a man again."

Pause. "Well, we are booked for the rest of the month. You can call back in September to see if you can come in," the receptionist says.

"Well, I may, but I will look for another doctor too."

"Oh," the receptionist says. "Whatever you want."

My stomach grips as though hungry. My younger sister Karen told me that since I was now forty, having regular physicals was very important.

"Well, I may call back."

"Fine," the receptionist says and hangs up.

I make a dash for the Internet and search for doctors. I pick up the phone and call my friend Marie who lives up the street whom I usually avoid because she always calls me to complain about something. She has a good doctor. When I called her, she was not home? I was praying that she had finally found a job.

My days of August are happy. I receive an African art book from my mom and another one from my sister for my birthday. My dad gives me a great greeting card that plays the music "Girls Just Wanna Have Fun" by Cyndi Lauper that used to be one of my favourite songs. I used to sing this song to him in my teens to annoy him. He would always smile. My eldest niece gives me a greeting card with her voice on it anchoring the news that there are so many candles on my birthday cake that there is a fire. My long-time friend Tiffany spends most of the day with me and we reminisce.

I eat McDonald's three times a day and exercise just about every day for thirty minutes on my treadmill in a corner of my apartment. I meet a beautiful new man. September comes at last.

Feeling inspired, early in September, I call Toronto Western Hospital's Family Health Team. The receptionist rebooks me with Dr. Toussaint and my appointment is later in the month.

I welcome the new graduate students at OISE/University of Toronto. I work at the OISE Student Success Centre. I continue to exercise for thirty minutes just about every day. I cut out McDonald's. My smoking is reaching almost two packs a day. My appointment is at ten thirty in the morning. No time to exercise on the Tuesday morning, I shower, wear black and jump in my car.

The best thing that morning is I find a parking spot that I pay thirty-six dollars for. At least I find a spot in the crowded lot. The next best thing, the beautiful black nurse with long gorgeous locks greets me as though we are old friends.

"Okay," she says. "First we need to take your blood pressure, your weight and your height."

We chat and laugh as she leads me to the machinery.

"You will need to take off your shoes," she says and sets up the equipment.

I raze down the zippers on both of my boot legs and slide out of them. I step on the scale: two hundred and twenty-five.

"I weigh myself sometimes at home," I say. "Sometimes I weigh in at two twenty."

The nurse says nothing to that.

"Okay, now we will need to take your height," she does say.

Feeling confident, I stand under the silver conductor's stick attached to a long pole with numbers. I can barely believe that after all these years, this is still how height is measured. I guess, if it ain't broke, don't fix it.

"Five-seven," the nurse says and removes the stick.

Man, that was not the music I wanted played. Something here needs to be fixed.

"I'm not five-seven," I say. "I have always been five-nine and a half."

The nurse says nothing to this.

"Okay, now your blood pressure," she does say.

It looks like that machine I see at Loblaws.

I sit and she wraps flat black plastic around my bare arms and seals it with Velcro. She pumps a black ball attached to the machine; numbers light up above our heads.

"That's not what we wanted to see," she says.

"What do you mean?" I ask.

"Well," she says. "Your numbers are here," she adds pointing to the one hundred and fifty, "we like to see them about twenty to thirty lowers than that."

I stare at these offensive numbers. "Oh," I say.

"You have high blood pressure," she says.

I hang my short head a little. "Well," I start with my eyes looking up at her, "I do smoke."

"Well," she says fast. "You are going to have to cut that out. Now you can see the doctor."

New life…I see a dietician at Loblaws for free who personally takes me around shopping with her. This morning I had oatmeal, with milk from my dad, four berries and fiber for breakfast. I plan to have the black beans and chickpeas mix with vegetables and a smidgen of four oils plus non-salt seasoning for lunch. I throw out all my sea salt and exercise for an hour each day. Still smoking, but my next physician's appointment is something I need to build up the courage to book. I really am five-nine and half and I buy measuring tape to prove it to myself. I am praying. I am working on it. The prayers work, as they always do. I have faith. Plus, now I am well under two hundred pounds. According to the doctor I saw at Toronto Western I am even under my ideal weight.

HEALTH

Gravity even works in the mouth

Have oatmeal, with four berries, strawberries, blackberries, raspberries and Blueberries for breakfast with fiber…some of it stuck to the roof of my mouth

Get my power toothbrush to get rid of it

Not all of it came off

Eventually, as I was waiting for Tiffany so we could go computer shopping for her, it comes down

Gravity works in the mouth

OUT OF HOSPITAL

Once I make the decision to keep taking my medication, the first thing I thought is that my days of dancing all night are over.

In the beginning I found two friends, Diane and Diane's friend Cheryl to spend time with. They both knew I was diagnosed with bipolar disorder and they both knew I was taking medication. At first, I did not change. I would go out dancing or to a bar, fill my body with margaritas and even bought margarita glasses from The Dollar Store with a light blue curvy and whirly stem. I bought a margarita shaker I still have to this day and would stir my own drinks.

Thanks to my psychiatrist, I stopped drinking and learned discipline. This was hard. Every night, faithfully, I would take my medication before I went to bed just as my doctor ordered. My father gave me the good advice to stick to one pharmacy to go to so they would maintain my records in case anything happened. I am fortunate to live in an area where there is a pharmacy close by, walking distance.

The medication I take is very, very sedating. I take three pink pills, a mood stabilizer, a green pill that is an anti-psychotic and half a milligram of clonazepam to combat anxiety. This stuff would make me sleep about sixteen hours. I struggled with this dilemma for about a year, missing out on morning interviews and good job opportunities and needing to do freelance work to facilitate the fact I could not wake up any earlier than 11:00 a.m.

At this time, I was living in a Toronto neighborhood called Parkdale. I went to see a young and extremely slender South Asian doctor there.

"You need to keep in mind the medication has a twelve-hour half-life. Whenever you want to wake up, take the medication twelve hours prior to that."

"What about my weight?" I asked. "I'm gaining weight."

"Don't eat," he said.

That was it, that simple, honestly, my problem was solved. I started to get a job with early morning hours easily after that, however due to the medication I found it hard not to eat. When I met Sean, he reintroduced me to great vitamins that I started to take. I started to regain more energy by eventually taking a multivitamin for sleep, five thousand milligrams of vitamin C for energy, calcium, D3, folic acid to prevent birth defects in case I ever became pregnant, vitamin E for my skin, Cold FX to protect myself from cold and flus on a daily basis, triple fish oil – six of them, pacific salmon oil, omega three-six-nine, a B complex to prevent stress, a drop of oregano oil under my tongue to get rid of the bloating to my belly, plus my medication. I may have even forgotten something. Thanks to seeing a physician at Toronto Western Hospital, I started to finally eat properly again and commit to exercising for thirty to sixty minutes daily. I do not see these things as having the time but needing the time to do these things for my health. My current battle to stop smoking is another hill to step over. I usually go to bed at a set time and I pray, keep happy thoughts in my head and avoid troubling things and troubling people. In this respect, I greatly believe in the song of Mary J. Blige, *No More Drama.*

Well, there is no more drama in my life. More than ten years out of the hospital with the words of my mother ringing in my ears if I ever feel as though something is disturbing my peace: "Don't ever let anything, or anyone drive you crazy."

BOOK LAUNCH

A manuscript I started in the nineteen nineties is a published book in 2007. I retain copyright and it is self-published with Lulu.com and on Amazon. In the winter of 2011, I take an expressive writing course at the University of Toronto. Encouraged to send a manuscript to the publisher, I send *Do Not Know*.

The book is about my battle with mental illness mainly in my twenties.

The publisher decides to go with it. We work on it for more than a year. During this time, I publish a story called "Lizard in the Yard" with the same publisher who is willing to re-publish *Do Not Know*.

As soon as the publisher finds out I am also doing a law degree and I negotiate intelligently over the contract, the books that my editor does have do not get sent to the book launch I even plan myself. The contract is not ever signed by me.

I self-publish the book the next day now called *How To Talk To Crazy People*. It is published on Lulu.com, Amazon Kindle, Amazon, iBookstore and Barnes & Noble, Kobo, Sony Reader as an eBook and/or as a paperback, in hardcover. There is also now an app available on the Apple Store.

BOOKS AND CDS BY DONNA KAKONGE

Headlight Anthology, Vol. 1
What Happened to the Afro?
How to Write Creative Non-fiction
Spiderwoman
My Roxanne
Being Healthy: Selected Works from the Internet (edited by)
Do Not Know
My Story of Transportation
Draft: eSpirituality Chats
Nine (CD)
Journalism Stories Collection
Digital Journals and Numerology
Matoke (Audio Download)
Spiderwoman (Audio Download)
In My Pocket
Where I Was
The Education Generation
Morning English Lessons
Radio and Television Announcing
Draft: Part Two
Ugandan Travelogue
School Works
Yes, School Works
School Works and Other Essays
Honest Psychic Chats
Story Ideas: Help For Writers' Block
Listening to Music
The Write Heart
This is How the Egyptians Fell
Natural Beauty

Stories in Red and Yellow: Digging Up Stories From Yesteryear
My Mind Book
Random Bibliography of Books and Internet Resources
The Best of Donna Magazine
Dropouts
Old Romance
How To Start Your Own Teaching and Writing Business
Smoking
The Adventures of a Canvas
Working on My Sleep
Love At A Distance
Teaching Curriculum Ideas
The Politics of Black Hair Online Coursebook
Radio Scripts
Lessons in Public Relations Issues
Totally Unknown Writers Festival Collection 2011
Natural and Colorful Beauty in Education
How To Talk To Crazy People
Young Black Women in Toronto High Schools (in progress)
Success (in progress)
No Fool No More (in progress)

ACKNOWLEGEMENTS

I would like to thank anyone and everyone who has ever believed in me and taken the time to get to know me.

ABOUT THREE QUARTERS

Teresa Madaleno reviews…
"Three Quarters" by Donna Kakonge

From the first chapter, *Three Quarters* manages to draw you in so that you sympathize with the main character who happens to be the author. She is just ten years old when we first meet her, and both the tone and writing style match her age. The innocent and tender language makes you feel as if this story is crafted by a child. As the young girl ages though, so does the method of expression. Suddenly the writing is too mature to be written by a child. There is a simple description of sitting on a bench at a mall with her siblings and another touching scene describing the day she brought her Dad to class, but then we move closer to current day and a harsher tone as author, Donna Kakonge describes the offensive language she encounters on a bus ride. Stark reality kicks in as she is reminded on that bus ride of a horrible incident from her childhood- Donna's innocence is lost and the writing turns candid.

How appropriate that the writing style transitions as the character ages. After all, *Three Quarters* is about growth and change. It traces the stages of the writer's life, including success and disappointments from childhood to present day. The story is often warm and tender. At other times it is frank.

The descriptive techniques the writer employs make it easy for the reader to imagine being present in the story. At one point, the writer is at a casino with her boyfriend and clearly wants out. She writes," I am tired of flittering around this crowded place like a refugee in a camp."

Like many young women, Donna must learn the hard way that people don't always live up to your expectations; life doesn't work out the way you plan. For example, the diamond engagement ring she receives in her thirties is a period of flight, fancy and adventure only to be followed by disappointment and heartache.

Three Quarters teaches us about innocence, reality, success, disappointment, kindness, and the mean-spirited. Each chapter is like a little morsel of life that can be consumed quickly by the reader who should only be too eager to move on to the next chapter. Three Quarters leaves you with just one burning question —What will happen in subsequent chapters of this lady's life?